Christmas in art and song

A collection of songs, carols and descriptive poems

Duke University Library

Christmas in art and song
A collection of songs, carols and descriptive poems

ISBN/EAN: 9783741190698

Manufactured in Europe, USA, Canada, Australia, Japa

Cover: Foto ©Andreas Hilbeck / pixelio.de

Manufactured and distributed by brebook publishing software
(www.brebook.com)

Christmas in art and song

CHRISTMAS

IN

ART AND SONG.

"Christmas
for
Ever!"

CHRISTMAS IN ART & SONG

NEW YORK

The Arundel
Printing & Pub. Co.

Nowell! Nowell! in this halle
Make mery, I praye nowe alle!
On that chyldē may wee calle.

    Ullo fine Crimine.

CHRISTMAS

IN

ART AND SONG:

A COLLECTION OF

Songs, Carols and Descriptive Poems,

RELATING TO THE

FESTIVAL OF CHRISTMAS.

ILLUSTRATED

FROM DRAWINGS BY DISTINGUISHED ARTISTS.

NEW YORK:
THE ARUNDEL PRINTING AND PUBLISHING COMPANY,
1879.

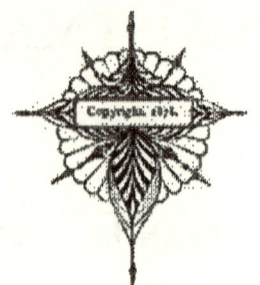

CONTENTS.

11

Contents.

ILLUSTRATIONS.

CHRISTMAS IN SONG—

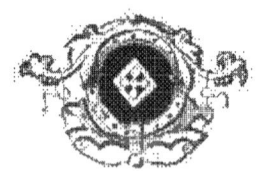

"Christ was Born

on

Christmas Day."

A CAROL.

WITH ILLUSTRATIONS BY JOHN A. HOWS.

Christ was born on Christmas
Day;
Wreathe the holly, twine the bay;
Christus natus hodie:

She gave the Son.
The Holy ONE of
Mary.

ECCE VIRGO CONCIPIET ET PARIET ALLELU

He is born
to set us free,
He is born our Lord to be,
Ex Maria Virgine;

GOD, the LORD,
By all adored for ever.
Yet the bright red berries glow
Everywhere in goodly show;
Christus natus hodie:

HAVE, the
SON,
the HOLY ONE
of Mary

Christian men, rejoice and
sing;
'Tis the birthday of a
King,
Ex Maria Virgine.

Agnus Dei

Agnus Dei

Qui tollis peccata mundi

Domine Fili Unigenite Jesu Christe

Qui tollis peccata mundi

Miserere nobis.

Dona nobis

GOD, the LORD,
By all adored
for ever.

Kyrie eleison.

Christe eleison

ight of sadness;
Morn of gladness
Evermore:
Over, Over:
After many troubles
sore,

Born of gladness, ever-
more and evermore.

Midnight scarcely passed
and over,
Drawing to this
holy morn,
Very early,
very early
Christ was born

Valley

Sharon & the Lily

The Rose of

Roll out with bliss,
His name is this:
EMMANUEL;
As was foretold
In days of old
By Gabriel.

Hosanna in Excelsis

CHRISTMAS IN SONG.

Christmas in the Olden Time.

(SIR WALTER SCOTT.)

HEAP on more wood!—the wind is chill;
But let it whistle as it will,
We'll keep our Christmas merry still.
Each age has deemed the new-born year
The fittest time for festal cheer.
And well our Christian sires of old
Loved when the year its course had rolled,
And brought blithe Christmas back again,
With all its hospitable train.
Domestic and religious rite
Gave honor to the holy night;
On Christmas eve the bells were rung;

Christmas in Art & Song.

On Christmas eve the mass was sung;
That only night, in all the year,
Saw the stoled priest the chalice rear.
The damsel donned her kirtle sheen;
The hall was dressed with holly green;
Forth to the wood did merry men go,
To gather in the mistletoe;
Then opened wide the baron's hall
To vassal, tenant, serf, and all;
Power laid his rod of rule aside,
And ceremony doffed his pride.
The heir, with roses in his shoes,
That night might village partner choose.
The lord, underognting, share
The vulgar game of " post and pair."
All hailed, with uncontrolled delight,
And general voice, the happy night,
That to the cottage, as the crown,
Brought tidings of salvation down.
The fire, with well-dried logs supplied,
Went roaring up the chimney wide;
The huge hall-table's oaken face,
Scrubbed till it shone, the day to grace,
Bore then upon its massive board
No mark to part the squire and lord.
Then was brought in the lusty brawn
By old blue-coated serving-man;
Then the grim boar's head frowned on high,
Crested with bays and rosemary.
Well can the green-garbed ranger tell
How, when, and where, the monster fell;
What dogs before his death he tore,
And all the baiting of the boar.

Christmas Alms-giving in the Olden Times.

The Wassail round, in good brown bowls,
Garnished with ribbons, blithely trowls.
There the huge sirloin reeked; hard by
Plum-porridge stood, and Christmas pie;
Nor failed old Scotland to produce,
At such high tide, her savory goose.
Then came the merry masquers in,
And carols roared with blithesome din;
If unmelodious was the song,
It was a hearty note, and strong.
Who lists may in their mumming see
Traces of ancient mystery;
White shirts supplied the masquerade,
And smutted cheeks the visors made;
But, O! what masquers, richly dight,
Can boast of bosoms half so light!
England was merry England, when
Old Christmas brought his sports again.
'Twas Christmas broached the mightiest ale;
'Twas Christmas told the merriest tale;
A Christmas gambol oft could cheer
The poor man's heart through half the year.

Christmas Comes but Once a Year.

(THOMAS MILLER.)

THOSE Christmas bells so sweetly chime,
    As on the day when first they rung
So merrily in the olden time,
    And far and wide their music flung:
Shaking the tall gray ivied tower,
With all their deep melodious power:
      They still proclaim to every ear,
      Old Christmas comes but once a year.

Then he came singing through the woods,
    And plucked the holly bright and green;
Pulled here and there the ivy buds;
    Was sometimes hidden, sometimes seen ---
Half-buried 'neath the mistletoe,
His long beard hung with flakes of snow;
      And still he ever carolled clear,
      Old Christmas comes but once a year.

He merrily came in days of old,
    When roads were few, and ways were foul;
Now staggered,—now some ditty trolled,
    Now drunk deep from his wassail-bowl :
His holly silvered o'er with frost
Nor ever once his way he lost,
      For reeling here and reeling there,
      Old Christmas comes but once a year.

The hall was then with holly crowned,
    'Twas on the wild deer's antlers placed;

It hemmed the battered armor round,
   And every ancient trophy graced.
It decked the boar's head, tusked and grim,
The wassail-bowl wreathed to the brim.
   A summer-green hung everywhere,
   For Christmas came but once a year.

His jaded steed the armèd knight
   Reined up before the abbey gate;
By all assisted to alight,
   From humble monk, to abbot great
They placed his lance behind the door,
His armor on the rush-strewn floor;
   And then brought out the best of cheer,
   For Christmas came but once a year.

The maiden then, in quaint attire,
　　Loosed from her head the silken hood,
And danced before the yule-clog fire—
　　The crackling monarch of the wood;
Helmet and shield flashed back the blaze
In lines of light, like summer rays,
　　While music sounded loud and clear;
　　For Christmas came but once a year.

What though upon his hoary head
　　Have fallen many a winter's snow,
His wreath is still as green and red
　　As 'twas a thousand years ago.
For what has he to do with care?
His wassail-bowl and old arm-chair
　　Are ever standing ready there,
　　For Christmas comes but once a year.

No marvel Christmas lives so long;
　　He never knew but merry hours;
His nights were spent with mirth and song.
　　In happy homes and princely bowers;
Was greeted both by serf and lord,
And seated at the festal board;
　　While every voice cried, "Welcome here."
　　Old Christmas comes but once a year.

But what care we for days of old,
　　The knights whose arms have turned to rust.
Their grim boars' heads, and pasties cold,
　　Their castles crumbled into dust?
Never did sweeter faces go,
Blushing beneath the mistletoe,

Than are to-night assembled here,
For Christmas still comes once a year.

For those old times are dead and gone,
 And those who hailed them passed away
Yet still there lingers many a one,
 To welcome in old Christmas Day.
The poor will many a care forget,
The debtor think not of his debt;
 But, as they each enjoy their cheer,
 Wish it was Christmas all the year.

And still around these good old times
 We hang like friends full loath to part,
We listen to the simple rhymes
 Which somehow sink into the heart,
" Half musical, half melancholy,"
Like childish smiles that still are holy ;
 A masquer's face dimmed with a tear,
 For Christmas comes but once a year.

The bells which usher in that morn,
 Have ever drawn my mind away
To Bethlehem, where Christ was born,
 And the low stable where He lay,
In which the large-eyed oxen fed ;
To Mary bowing low her head,
 And looking down with love sincere ;
 Such thoughts bring Christmas once a year

At early day the youthful voice,
 Heard singing on from door to door,
Makes the responding heart rejoice,

To know the children of the poor
For once are happy all day long;
We smile and listen to the song,
   The burden still remote or near,
    "Old Christmas comes but once a year."

Upon a gayer, happier scene,
   Never did holly berries peer,
Or ivy throw its trailing green.
   On brighter forms than there are here,
Nor Christmas in his old arm-chair
Smile upon lips and brows more fair:
   Then let us sing amid our cheer,
   Old Christmas still comes once a year.

Christmas is Come.

(ALBERT SMITH.)

THE old north breeze through the skeleton trees
   Is chanting the year out drearily;
But loud let it blow, for at home we know
   That the dry logs crackle cheerily;
And the frozen ground is in fetters bound;
   But pile up the wood, we can burn it;
For Christmas is come, and in every home
   To summer our hearts can turn it
    Wassail! wassail!
Here's happiness to all, abroad and at home;
    Wassail! wassail!
Here's happiness to all, for Christmas is come.

And far and near, o'er landscape drear,
   From casements brightly streaming,
With cheerful glow on the fallen snow
   The ruddy light is gleaming;
The wind may shout as it likes without,
   It may bluster, but never can harm us;
For a merrier din shall resound within,
   And our Christmas feelings warm us.
       Wassail! wassail!
Here's happiness to all, abroad and at home;
       Wassail! wassail!
Here's happiness to all, for Christmas is come.

The flowers are torpid in their beds,
   Till spring's first sunbeam sleeping;
Not e'en the snowdrops' pointed heads
   Along the earth are peeping;
But groves remain on each frosted pane
   Of feathery trees and bowers;
And fairer far we'll maintain they are
   Than summer's gaudiest flowers.
       Wassail! wassail!
Here's happiness to all, abroad and at home;
       Wassail! wassail!
Here's happiness to all, for Christmas is come.

Let us drink to those eyes we most dearly prize,
   We can show how we love them after;
The fire blaze cleaves to the bright holly leaves,
   And the mistletoe hangs from the rafter;
We care not for fruit, whilst we here can see
   Their scarlet and pearly berries;

For the girls' soft cheeks shall our peaches be,
And their pouting lips our cherries.
Wassail! wassail!
Here's happiness to all, abroad and at home;
Wassail! wassail!
Here's happiness to all, for Christmas is come.

————•————

Christmas Time.

(JOHN CLARE.)

GLAD Christmas comes, and every hearth
Makes room to give him welcome now,
E'en want will dry its tears in mirth,
And crown him with a holly bough;
Though tramping 'neath a winter sky,
O'er snowy paths and rimy stiles,
The housewife sets her spinning by,
To bid him welcome with her smiles.

Each house is swept the day before,
And windows stuck with evergreens;
The snow is besomed from the door,
And comfort crowns the cottage scenes.
Gilt holly with its thorny pricks,
And yew, and box, with berries small,
These deck the unused candlesticks,
And pictures hanging by the wall.

Neighbors resume their annual cheer,
Wishing, with smiles and spirits high,

Christmas Time.

Glad Christmas and a happy year,
  To every morning passer-by;
Milkmaids their Christmas journeys go,

Accompanied by a favored swain;
And children pace the crumpling snow,
  To taste their granny's cake again.

Christmas in Art & Song.

The shepherd now no more afraid,
  Since custom doth the chance bestow,
Starts up to kiss the giggling maid,
  Beneath the branch of mistletoe,
That 'neath each cottage beam is seen,
  With pearl-like berries shining gay;
The shadow still of what hath been,
  Which fashion yearly fades away.

The singing waits—a merry throng,
  At early morn, with simple skill,
Yet imitate the angel's song,
  And chant their Christmas ditty still;
And, 'mid the storm that dies and swells
  By fits, in hummings softly steals
The music of the village bells,
  Ringing around their merry peals.

When this is past, a merry crew,
  Bedecked in masks and ribbons gay,
The Morris Dance, their sports renew,
  And act their winter evening play.
The clown turned king, for penny praise,
  Storms with the actor's strut and swell,
And harlequin, a laugh to raise,
  Wears his hunch-back and tinkling bell.

And oft for pence and spicy ale,
  With winter nosegays pinned before,
The wassail-singer tells her tale,
  And drawls her Christmas carols o'er.
While 'prentice boy, with ruddy face,
  And rime-bepowdered dancing locks,

From door to door, with happy face,
   Runs round to claim his "Christmas-box."

The block upon the fire is put,
   To sanction custom's old desires,
And many a fagot's bands are cut,
   For the old farmer's Christmas fires,
Where loud-tongued gladness joins the throng,
   And Winter meets the warmth of May,
Till, feeling soon the heat too strong,
   He rubs his shins and draws away.

While snows the window-panes bedim,
   The fire curls up a sunny charm,
Where, creaming o'er the pitcher's rim,
   The flowering ale is set to warm.
Mirth, full of joy as summer bees,
   Sits there its pleasures to impart,
And children, 'tween their parents' knees,
   Sing scraps of carols off by heart.

And some, to view the winter weathers,
   Climb up the window seat with glee,
Likening the snow to falling feathers,
   In fancy's infant ecstacy;
Laughing, with superstitious love,
   O'er visions wild that youth supplies,
Of people pulling geese above,
   And keeping Christmas in the skies.

As though the homestead trees were drest,
   In lieu of snow, with dancing leaves,
As though the sun-dried martin's nest,

Instead of io'cles hung the eaves;
The children hail the happy day—
  As if the snow were April's grass,
And pleased, as 'neath the warmth of May,
  Sport o'er the water froze to glass.

Thou day of happy sound and mirth
  That long with childish memory stays,
How blest around the cottage hearth,
  I met thee in my younger days,
Harping, with rapture's dreaming joys,
  On presents which thy coming found,
The welcome sight of little toys,
  The Christmas gift of cousins round.

About the glowing hearth at night,
  The harmless laugh and winter tale
Go round; while parting friends delight
  To toast each other o'er their ale.
The cotter oft with quiet zeal
  Will, musing. o'er his Bible lean;
While, in the dark the lovers steal,
  To kiss and toy behind the screen.

Old customs! O! I love the sound,
  However simple they may be;
Whate'er with time hath sanction found,
  Is welcome, and is dear to me;
Pride grows above simplicity,
  And spurns them from her haughty mind:
And soon the poet's song will be
  The only refuge they can find.

Old Christmas.

(J. BRIDGMAN.)

Once more the rapid, fleeting year
  Has brought old Christmas to the door;
Come, let us treat him with such cheer.
  As folks were wont in days of yore,
When burgher grave, and belted knight.
  And cottage maid, and lady fair,
Obeyed the old familiar sprite,
  And, at his bidding, banished Care—
That sullen, surly, melancholy wight.

Let's hang from beams all black with time,
  The mistletoe's insidious bough,
'Neath which, as little birds with lime,
  Young girls are snared, "they know not how
The horrid thing—they never thought
  It half so near—for if they had,
'Tis certain they had not been caught—
  On that rely—it was too bad,
And not at all behaving as one ought."

Upon the hearth pile up the fire,
  And, that it may burn clear and bright,
Cast in it every base desire,
  All envy, hatred, vengeance, spite;
Believe me, the event will show
  By acting in this way you'll gain—
For you will feel a genial glow
  Dance through each gladly-swelling vein,
And onwards to your very heart's core go.

Bring, too, the sparkling wassail-bowl,
 That jolly Christmas holds so dear,
And if you'd have it warm your soul—
 The mind as well as body cheer—
Amid the wine and spirit pour
 The blessings from some humble roof;
A little charity is sure
 To call them forth; in sober truth,
They'll give the draught one matchless flavor more.

And you, fair Sovereign of this isle,
 Who love to deck the Christmas tree,
So that the massy, regal pile
 Resound with mirth and jollity,
Remember that the stem with new
 Strength thrives, if pruned with careful hand,
Then trim your Christmas sapling, too,
 And to the poor throughout the land
Send of the shoots thus lopped away a few.

— ·

Christmas Tide.

(ELIZA COOK.)

WHEN the merry spring-time weaves
 Its peeping bloom and dewy leaves;
When the primrose opes its eye,
 And the young moth flutters by;
When the plaintive turtle-dove
 Pours its notes of peace and love;
And the clear sun flings its glory bright and wide—

Yet my soul will own
More joy in winter's frown,
And wake with warmer flush at Christmas tide.

The summer beams may shine
On the rich and curling vine,
And the noontide rays light up
The tulip's dazzling cup;
But the pearly mistletoe,
And the holly berries' glow,
Are not even by the boasted rose outvied ;
For the happy hearths beneath
The green and coral wreath
Love the garlands that are twined at Christmas tide.

Let the autumn days produce
Yellow corn and purple juice,
And Nature's feast be spread
In the fruitage ripe and red ;
'Tis grateful to behold
Gushing grapes, and fields of gold,
When cheeks are browned, and red lips deeper dyed ;
But give, oh ! give to me,
The winter night of glee,
The mirth and plenty seen at Christmas tide.

The northern gust may howl,
The rolling storm-cloud scowl,
King Frost may make a slave
Of the river's rapid wave ;
The snow-drift choke the path,
Or the hail-shower spend its wrath,

But the sternest blast right bravely is defied,
   While limbs and spirits bound
   To the merry minstrel sound,
And social wood-fires blaze at Christmas tide.

   The song, the laugh, the shout,
   Shall mock the storm without;
   And the sparkling wine-foam rise
   'Neath still more sparkling eyes;
   The forms that scarcely meet
   Then hand to hand shall greet,
And soul pledge soul that leagues too long divide.
   Mirth, friendship, love, and light,
   Shall crown the winter night,
And every glad voice welcome Christmas tide.

   But while joy's echo falls
   In gay and plenteous halls,
   Let the poor and lowly share
   The warmth, the sports, the fare;
   For the one of humble lot
   Must not shiver in his cot,
But claim a bounteous meed from wealth and pride.
   Shed kindly blessings round,
   Till no aching heart be found,
And then all hail to merry Christmas tide!

Christmas Minstrelsy.

ADDRESSED TO THE REV. DR. WORDSWORTH.

(WILLIAM WORDSWORTH.)

THE Minstrels played their Christmas tune
  To-night beneath my cottage eaves;
While, smitten by a lofty moon,
  The encircling laurels, thick with leaves,
Gave back a rich and dazzling sheen,
That overpowered their natural green.

Through hill and valley every breeze
    Had sunk to rest with folded wings:
Keen was the air, but could not freeze,
    Nor check the music of the strings;
So stout and hardy were the band
That scraped the chords with strenuous hand!

And who but listened?—till was paid
    Respect to every inmate's claim:
The greeting given, the music played,
    In honor of each household name,
Duly pronounced with lusty call,
And "merry Christmas" wished to all!

O brother! I revere the choice
    That took thee from thy native hills;
And it is given thee to rejoice:
    Though public care full often tills
(Heaven only witness of the toil)
A barren and ungrateful soil.

Yet, would that thou, with me and mine,
    Hadst heard this never-failing rite;
And seen on other faces shine
    A true revival of the light,
Which Nature and these rustic powers,
In simple childhood, spread through ours!

For pleasure hath not ceased to wait
    On these expected annual rounds;
Whether the rich man's sumptuous gate
    Call forth the unelaborate sounds,
Or they are offered at the door
That guards the lowliest of the poor.

Christmas in Art & Song.

How touching, when, at midnight, sweep
  Snow-muffled winds, and all is dark,
To hear—and sink again to sleep!
  Or, at an earlier call, to mark,
By blazing fire, the still suspense
Of self-complacent innocence!

The mutual nod,—the grave disguise
  Of hearts with gladness brimming o'er;
And some unbidden tears that rise
  For names once heard, and heard no more;
Tears brightened by the serenade
For infant in the cradle laid.

Ah! not for emerald fields alone,
  With ambient streams more pure and bright
Than fabled Cytherea's zone
  Glittering before the Thunderer's sight,
Is to my heart of hearts endeared
The ground where we were born and reared!

Hail, ancient Manners! sure defence,
  Where they survive, of wholesome laws;
Remnants of love whose modest sense
  Thus into narrow room withdraws;
Hail, Usages of pristine mould,
And ye that guard them, Mountains old!

Bear with me, brother! quench the thought
  That slights this passion, or condemns;
If thee fond Fancy ever brought
  From the proud margin of the Thames,
And Lambeth's venerable towers,
To humbler streams and greener bowers.

Knighting the Loin of Beef.

Yes, they can make, who fail to find,
  Short leisure even in busiest days,
Moments to cast a look behind,
  And profit by those kindly rays
That through the clouds do sometimes steal,
And all the far-off past reveal.

Hence, while the imperial City's din
  Beats frequent on thy satiate ear,
A pleased attention I may win
  To agitations less severe,
That neither overwhelm nor cloy,
But fill the hollow vale with joy!

— ➤ —

The Knighting of the Sirloin of Beef by Charles the Second.

The Second CHARLES of England
  Rode forth one Christmas tide,
To hunt a gallant stag of ten,
  Of Chingford woods the pride.

The wind blew keen, the snow fell fast,
  And made for earth a pall,
As tired steeds and wearied men
  Returned to Friday Hall.

The blazing logs, piled on the dogs,
  Were pleasant to behold!
And grateful was the steaming feast
  To hungry men—and cold.

Knighting the Loin of Beef

Wassail.

With right good-will all took their fill,
    And soon each found relief;
Whilst Charles his royal trencher piled
    From one huge loin of beef.

Quoth Charles, "Odd's fish! a noble dish!
    Aye, noble made by me!
By kingly right, I dub thee knight—
    Sir Loin henceforward be!"

And never was a royal jest
    Received with such "acclaim:"
And never knight than good Sir Loin
    More worthy of the name.

Wassail.

Wassail! wassail! Ye merry men, hail,
    Who brightened the days of old;
What brave conceits, and humorsome feats,
    Are sung of our fathers bold!
From morning chime, unto vesper time,
    They revelled in careless glee,
And danced at night with spirits as light
    As the notes of their minstrelsy.

Wassail! wassail! At the knight's regale
    'Twas the signal for deep carouse,
Nor there alone, for the joyous tone
    Shook many a priestly house;

The monks forgot their bachelor's lot,
 Surrounded by goodly cheer,
And raised the cup, in its brim full up,
 To the utter contempt of care.

Wassail! wassail! cried the yeoman hale,
 As he shouldered his quarter-staff,
And homeward rode where the spiced ale stood
 Awaiting his hearty quaff;
The cot meanwhile, lit up by the smile
 Of a frank, good-hearted mirth,
And free to all who might chance to call,
 Was the happiest place on earth!

The Mahogany Tree.

The Mahogany Tree.

(W. M. THACKERAY.)

CHRISTMAS is here;
Winds whistle shrill,
Icy and chill:
Little care we.
Little we fear
Weather without,
Sheltered about
The Mahogany Tree.

Commoner greens,
Ivy and oaks,
Poets, in jokes,
Sing, do you see:
Good fellows' shins
Here, boys, are found,
Twisting around
The Mahogany Tree.

Once on the boughs
Birds of rare plume
Sang, in its bloom:
Night birds are we;
Here we carouse,
Singing, like them,
Perched round the stem
Of the jolly old tree.

Here let us sport,
Boys, as we sit;
Laughter and wit
Flashing so free.
Life is but short—
When we are gone,
Let them sing on,
Round the old tree.

Evenings we knew,
Happy as this;
Faces we miss,
Pleasant to see.
Kind hearts and true,
Gentle and just,
Peace to your dust!
We sing round the tree.

Care, like a dun,
Lurks at the gate:
Let the dog wait;
Happy we'll be!
Drink every one;
Pile up the coals,
Fill the red bowls,
Round the old tree!

Drain we the cup.—
Friend, art afraid?
Spirits are laid
In the Red Sea.
Mantle it up;
Empty it yet;
Let us forget,
Round the old tree.

Sorrows, begone!
Life and its ills,
Duns and their bills,
Bid we to flee.
Come with the dawn
Blue-devil sprite,
Leave us to-night,
Round the old tree.

The Approach of Christmas.

(JOHN GAY.)

WHEN rosemary, and bays, the poets' crown.
Are bawled, in frequent cries, through all the town;
Then judge the festival of Christmas near,—
Christmas, the joyous period of the year.
Now with bright holly all your temples strew,
With laurel green, and sacred mistletoe;
Now, heaven-born Charity! thy blessings shed;
Bid meagre Want uprear her sickly head;

The Mistletoe.

Bid shivering limbs be warm; let Plenty's bowl
In humble roofs make glad the needy soul!
See, see! the heaven-born maid her blessings shed;
Lo! meagre Want uprears her sickly head;
Clothed are the naked, and the needy glad,
While selfish Avarice alone is sad.

The Mistletoe.

(BARRY CORNWALL.)

WHEN winter nights grow long,
  And winds without blow cold,
We sit in a ring round the warm wood fire,
  And listen to stories old!
And we try to look grave (as maids should be),
When the men bring in boughs of the laurel-tree.
    O, the laurel, the evergreen tree!
    The poets have laurels, and why not we?

How pleasant, when night falls down,
  And hides the wintry sun,
To see them come in to the blazing fire,
  And know that their work is done;
Whilst many bring in, with a laugh or rhyme,
Green branches of holly for Christmas time.
    O, the holly, the bright green holly!
    It tells (like a tongue) that the times are jolly!

Sometimes—(in our grave house
  Observe, this happeneth not;)

But at times the evergreen laurel boughs,
    And the holly are all forgot,
And then—what then? why, the men laugh low,
And hang up a branch of—the mistletoe!
        Oh, brave is the laurel! and brave is the holly.
        But the mistletoe banisheth melancholy!
        Ah, nobody knows, nor ever *shall* know,
        What is done under the mistletoe.

——— • ———

The Christmas Holly.

(ELIZA COOK.)

The holly! the holly! oh, twine it with bay—
    Come give the holly a song;
For it helps to drive stern winter away,
    With his garment so sombre and long;
It peeps through the trees with its berries of red,
    And its leaves of burnished green,
When the flowers and fruits have long been dead,
    And not even the daisy is seen.
Then sing to the holly, the Christmas holly,
    That hangs over peasant and king;
While we laugh and carouse 'neath its glittering boughs,
    To the Christmas holly we'll sing.

The gale may whistle, the frost may come
    To fetter the gurgling rill;
The woods may be bare, and warblers dumb,
    But holly is beautiful still.
In the revel and light of princely halls
    The bright holly branch is found;

And its shadow falls on the lowliest walls,
  While the brimming horn goes round.
Then drink to the holly, &c.

The ivy lives long, but its home must be
  Where graves and ruins are spread;
There's beauty about the cypress tree,
  But it flourishes near the dead;
The laurel the warrior's brow may wreathe,
  But it tells of tears and blood;
I sing the holly, and who can breathe
  Aught of that that is not good?
Then sing to the holly, &c.

The Holly Berry.

(THOMAS MILLER.)

Gone are the summer hours,
  The birds have left their bowers;
While the holly true retains his hue,
  Nor changes like the flowers.
On his armèd leaf reposes
  The berries tinged like roses;
For he's ever seen in red or green,
  While grim old Winter dozes.
    Then drink to the holly berry,
    With hey down, hey down derry;
    The mistletoe we'll pledge also,
    And at Christmas all be merry.

Above all cold affections,
Like pleasant recollections,
The ivy grows, and a deep veil throws
O'er all Time's imperfections;
The mould'ring column screening,
The naked gateway greening,
While the falling shrine it doth entwine
Like a heart that's homeward leaning.
    Then drink, &c.

We read in ancient story,
How the Druids in their glory
Marched forth of old, with hooks of gold,
To forests dim and hoary;
The giant oak ascended,
Then from its branches rended
The mistletoe, long long ago,
By maidens fair attended.
    Then drink, &c.

Each thorpe and grange surrounding,
The waits to music bounding,
Aroused the cook, that her fire might smoke
Ere the early cock was sounding.
For all the land was merry,
And rang with "Hey down derry,"
While in castle hall, and cottage small,
There glittered the holly berry.
    Then drink, &c.

Holly Song.

(WILLIAM SHAKSPEARE.)

BLOW, blow, thou winter wind,
　Thou art not so unkind
　　As man's ingratitude;
　Thy tooth is not so keen,
　Because thou art not seen,
　　Although thy breath be rude.

Heigh, ho! sing heigh, ho! unto the green holly:
Most friendship is feigning, most loving mere folly:
　　Then, heigh, ho! the holly!
　　This life is most jolly.

Freeze, freeze, thou bitter sky,
Thou dost not bite so nigh
As benefits forgot:
Though thou the waters warp,
Thy sting is not so sharp
As friend remembered not.
Heigh, ho! sing heigh, ho! unto the green holly:
Most friendship is feigning, most loving mere folly:
Then, heigh, ho! the holly!
This life is most jolly.

Church-Decking at Christmas.

(WILLIAM WORDSWORTH.)

WOULD that our scrupulous sires had dared to leave
Less scanty measure of those graceful rites
And usages, whose due return invites
A stir of mind too natural to deceive;
Giving the memory help when she could weave
A crown for Hope!—I dread the boasted lights
That all too often are but fiery blights,
Killing the bud o'er which in vain we grieve.
Go, seek, when Christmas snows discomfort bring,
The counter Spirit found in some gay church
Green with fresh holly, every pew a perch
In which the linnet or the thrush might sing,
Merry and loud, and safe from prying search,
Strains offered only to the genial spring.

Old English Carols.

Boar's Head Carols,

I.

TIDINGS I bring you for to tell
What in wild forest me befell,
When I in with a wild beast fell,
   With a boar so bryme.*

A boar so bryme that me pursued,
Me for to kill so sharply moved,—
That brymly beast, so cruel and rude,
    There tamed I him,
And reft from him both life and limb

    * Fierce.

Truly, to show you this is true,
His head I with my sword did hew,
To make this day new mirth for you—

Now eat thereof anon.
Eat, and much good do it you;
Take you bread and mustard thereto.
Joy with me that this I have done,
I pray you be glad every one,
 And all rejoice as one.

II.

Nowel, Nowel, Nowel, Nowel,
Tidings good I think to tell.

The boar's head, that we bring here,
Betokeneth a prince without peer
Is born to-day to buy us dear,
 Nowel.

The boar he is a sovereign beast,
And acceptable at every feast;
So might this lord be to greatest and least;
 . Nowel.

This boar's head we bring with song,
In worship of Him that thus sprung
From a virgin to redress all wrong;
 Nowel.

III.

At the beginning of the meat
Of a boar's head ye shall eat,
And in the mustard ye shall whet;
 And ye shall sing before ye go.

Welcome be ye that are here,
Ye shall all have right good cheer,
And also a right good fare;
   And ye shall sing before ye go.

Welcome be ye every one,
For ye shall sing all right anon;
Hey! you sure that ye have done?
   And ye shall sing before ye go.

IV.

    HEY! Hey! Hey! Hey!
     The boar's head is armèd gay.

THE boar's head in hand I bring,
With garlands gay encircling,*
I pray you all with me to sing,
     With Hey!

Lords, knights, and squires,
Parsons, priests, and vicars,
The boar's head is the first mess,†
     With Hey!

The boar's head, as I now say,
Takes its leave and goes away,
Goeth after the Twelfth day,
     With Hey!

Then comes in the second course with great pride,
The cranes, the herons, the bitterns, by their side,

---

* "Porttorying" in the original—a word not explained in any glossary.
† That is, "the first dish."

The partridges, the plovers, the woodcocks, and the snipe,
Larks in hot show, for the ladies to pick,
Good drink also, luscious and fine,
Blood of Allemaine, romnay, and wine,
                                        With Hey!

Good brewed ale and wine, I dare well say,
The boar's head with mustard armed so gay,
Furmity for pottage, and venison fine,
And the umbles of the doe and all that ever comes in.
Capons well baked, with knuckles of the roe,
Raisons and currants, and other spices too,
                                        With Hey!

V.

Caput Apri defero
Reddens laudes Domino.

THE boar's head in hand bring I,
With garlands gay and rosemary;
I pray you all sing merrily,
    Qui estis in convivio.

The boar's head, I understand,
Is the chief service in this land;
Look wherever it be found,
    Servite cum cantico.

Be glad, lords, both more or less,
    For this hath ordained our steward
To cheer you all this Christmas,
    The boar's head with mustard.

VI.

THE Boar is dead,
Lo, here is his head :
    What man could have done more
Than his head off to strike,
Meleager like,
    And bring it as I do before?

Ho living spoiled
Where good men toiled,
    Which made kind Ceres sorry ;
But now, dead and drawn,
Is very good brawn,
    And we have brought it for ye.

Then set down the swineyard,
The foe to the vineyard,
   Let Bacchus crown his fall;
Let this boar's head and mustard
Stand for pig, goose, and custard,
   And so you are welcome all.

———

A Carol for a Wassail Bowl.

A JOLLY Wassail Bowl,
   A Wassail of good ale,
Well fare the butler's soul,
   That setteth this to sale—
      Our jolly Wassail.

Good dame, here at your door
   Our Wassail we begin,
We are all maidens poor.
   We now pray let us in,
      With our Wassail.

Our Wassail we do fill
   With apples and with spice,
Then grant us your good-will,
   To taste here once or twice
      Of our Wassail.

If any maidens be
    Here dwelling in this house,
They kindly will agree
    To take a full carouse
            Of our Wassail.

But here they let us stand
    All freezing in the cold;
Good master, give command
    To enter and be bold,
            With our Wassail.

Much joy into this hall
    With us is entered in,
Our master first of all,
    We hope will now begin,
            Of our Wassail.

And after, his good wife
    Our spiced bowl will try,—
The Lord prolong your life!
    Good fortune we espy,
            For our Wassail.

Some bounty from your hands,
    Our Wassail to maintain:
We'll buy no house nor lands
    With that which we do gain,
            With our Wassail.

This is our merry night
    Of choosing King and Queen,
Then be it your delight
    That something may be seen
            In our Wassail.

It is a noble part
 To bear a liberal mind;
God bless our master's heart!
 For here we comfort find,
   With our Wassail.

And now we must be gone,
 To seek out more good cheer;
Where bounty will be shown,
 As we have found it here,
   With our Wassail.

Much joy betide them all,
 Our prayers shall be still,
We hope, and ever shall.
 For this your great good-will
   To our Wassail.

———

Ceremony for Christmas Eve.

Come bring with a noise,
My merry, merry boys,
The Christmas log to the firing,
 While my good dame, she
 Bids ye all be free,
And drink to your heart's desiring.

Ceremony for Christmas Eve.

With the last year's brand
Light the new block, and
For good success in his spending,

On your psalteries play,
That sweet luck may
Come while the log is a tending.

Drink now the strong beer,
Cut the white loaf here,
The while the meat is a shredding
For the rare mince-pie,
And the plums stand by,
To fill the paste that's a kneading.

"In Excelsis Gloria."

WHEN Christ was born of Mary free,
In Bethlehem, in that fair citie,
Angels sang there with mirth and glee,
In Excelsis Gloria!

Herdsmen beheld these angels bright,
To them appearing with great light,
Who said, "God's Son is born this night."
In Excelsis Gloria!

This King is come to save mankind,
As in Scripture truths we find,
Therefore this song have we in mind,
In Excelsis Gloria!

Then, dear Lord, for Thy great grace,
Grant us the bliss to see Thy face,
That we may sing to Thy solace,
In Excelsis Gloria!

Religious Poems.

A Hymn on the Nativity of my Saviour.

(BEN JONSON.)

I SING the birth was born to-night,
The Author both of life and light;
    The angels so did sound it,
And like the ravished shepherds said,
Who saw the light and were afraid,
    Yet searched, and true they found it.

The Son of God, th' Eternal King,
That did us all salvation bring,
    And freed the soul from danger;
He whom the whole world could not take,
The Word, which heaven and earth did make,
    Was now laid in a manger.

The Father's wisdom willed it so,
The Son's obedience knew no No,
    Both wills were in one stature;
And as that wisdom had decreed,
The Word was now made Flesh indeed,
    And took on him our nature.

What comfort by Him do we win,
Who made Himself the price of sin,
 To make us heirs of Glory!
To see this babe, all innocence,
A martyr born in our defence:
 Can man forget this story?

———— • ————

For Christmas Day.

(BISHOP HALL.)

IMMORTAL Babe, who this dear day
Didst change Thine heaven for our clay,
And didst with flesh Thy godhead veil,
Eternal Son of God, all hail!

Shine, happy star; ye angels, sing
Glory on high to Heaven's King.
Run, shepherds, leave your nightly watch;
See Heaven come down to Bethlehem's cratch.

Worship, ye sages of the East,
The King of God in meanness dressed.
O, blessed maid! smile and adore
The God thy womb and arms have bore.

Star, angels, shepherds, and wild sages,
Thou virgin glory of all ages,
Restor'd frame of Heaven and Earth,
Joy in your dear Redeemer's birth!

MADONNA AND CHILD BY RAPHAEL.

Christmas.

(GEORGE HERBERT.)

ALL after pleasures as I rid one day,
　My horse and I, both tired, body and mind,
With full cry of affections, quite astray,
　I took up in the next inn I could find;
There when I came, whom found I but my dear,
　My dearest Lord, expecting till the grief
Of pleasures brought me to Him, ready there
　To be all passengers' most sweet relief?
O Thou, whose glorious, yet contracted light,
　Wrapt in night's mantle, stole into a manger;
Since my dark soul and brutish is Thy right,
　To man of all beasts be not Thou a stranger:
Furnish and deck my soul, that Thou mayst have
A better lodging, than a rack or grave.

The shepherds sing; and shall I silent be?
　My God, no hymn for Thee?
My soul's a shepherd too; a flock it feeds
　Of thoughts, and words, and deeds.
The pasture is Thy words; the streams, Thy grace
　Enriching all the place.
Shepherd and flock shall sing, and all my powers
　Outsing the daylight hours.
Then we will chide the sun for letting night
　Take up his place and right:
We sing one common Lord; wherefore He should
　Himself the candle hold.

I will go searching, till I find a sun
    Shall stay till we have done;
A willing shiner, that shall shine as gladly,
    As frost-night suns look sadly.
Then we will sing, and shine all our own day,
    And one another pay:
His beams shall cheer my breast, and both so twine,
Till e'en his beams sing, and my music shine.

Of Christ's Birth in an Inn.

(JEREMY TAYLOR.)

THE blessèd Virgin travailed without pain,
    And lodgèd in an inn,
    A glorious star the sign,
But of a greater guest than ever came that way,
    For there He lay
That is the God of night and day,
And over all the pow'rs of heav'n doth reign.
It was the time of great Augustus' tax,
    And then He comes
    That pays all sums,
Even the whole price of lost humanity;
    And sets us free
    From the ungodly emperie
Of Sin, of Satan, and of Death.
O, make our hearts, blest God, Thy lodging-place,
    And in our breast
    Be pleased to rest.

For Thou lov'st temples better than an inn,
  And cause that Sin
May not profane the Deity within,
And sully o'er the ornaments of grace.

——— - ——

Hymn to the Nativity.

(JOHN MILTON.)

It was the winter wild,
 While the heaven-born Child
All meanly wrapt in the rude manger lies:
 Nature, in awe to Him,
 Had doffed her gaudy trim,
With her great Master so to sympathize:
It was no season then for her
To wanton with the sun, her lusty paramour.

 Only with speeches fair
 She woos the gentle air,
To hide her guilty front with innocent snow;
 And on her naked shame,
 Pollute with sinful blame,
The saintly veil of maiden white to throw;
Confounded, that her Maker's eyes
Should look so near upon her foul deformities.

 But He, her fears to cease,
 Sent down the meek-eyed Peace;
She, crowned with olive green, came softly sliding

The Nativity, by Rubens

Down through the turning sphere,
His ready harbinger,
With turtle wing the amorous cloud dividing;
And, waving wide her myrtle wand,
She strikes a universal peace through sea and land.

No war, or battle's sound,
Was heard the world around:
The idle spear and shield were high up hung;
The hookèd chariot stood
Unstained with hostile blood;
The trumpet spake not to the armèd throng:
And kings sat still with awful eye,
As if they surely knew their sovereign Lord was by.

But peaceful was the night,
Wherein the Prince of Light
His reign of peace upon the earth began:
The winds, with wonder whist,
Smoothly the waters kissed,
Whispering new joys to the mild ocean
Who now hath quite forgot to rave,
While birds of calm sit brooding on the charmèd wave.

The stars, with deep amaze,
Stand fixed in steadfast gaze,
Bending one way their precious influence;
And will not take their flight,
For all the morning light,
Or Lucifer that often warned them thence;
But in their glimmering orbs did glow,
Until their Lord Himself bespake, and bid them go.

And, though the shady gloom
    Had given day her room,
The sun himself withheld his wonted speed,
    And hid his head for shame,
    As his inferior flame
The new enlightened world no more should need :
He saw a greater Sun appear
Than his bright throne, or burning axletree, could bear.

    The shepherds on the lawn,
    Or ere the point of dawn,
Sat simply chatting in a rustic row :
    Full little thought they then,
    That the mighty Pan
Was kindly come to live with them below ;
Perhaps their loves, or else their sheep,
Was all that did their silly thoughts so busy keep

    When such music sweet
    Their hearts and ears did greet,
As never was by mortal finger strook ;
    Divinely warbled voice
    Answering the stringed noise,
As all their souls in blissful rapture took :
The air, such pleasure loath to lose,
With thousand echoes still prolongs each heavenly close.

    Nature, that heard such sound,
    Beneath the hollow round
Of Cynthia's seat, the airy region thrilling,
    Now was almost won
    To think her part was done,

And that her reign had here its last fulfilling;
She knew such harmony alone
Could hold all heaven and earth in happier union.

At last surrounds their sight
A globe of circular light,
That with long beams the shame-faced night arrayed;
The helmèd cherubim,
And sworded seraphim,
Are seen in glittering ranks with wings displayed,
Harping in loud and solemn choir,
With unexpressive notes, to Heaven's new-born Heir.

Such music (as 'tis said)
Before was never made,

But when of old the sons of morning sung,
    While the Creator great
    His constellations set,
And the well-balanced world on hinges hung;
    And cast the dark foundations deep,
And bid the weltering waves their oozy channel keep.

    Ring out, ye crystal spheres,
    Once bless our human ears,
If ye have power to touch our senses so;
    And let your silver chime
    Move in melodious time;
And let the bass of heaven's deep organ blow;
    And with your ninefold harmony,
Make up full consort to the angelic symphony.

    For, if such holy song
    Enwrap our fancy long,
Time will run back and fetch the age of gold;
    And speckled vanity
    Will sicken soon and die,
And leprous sin will melt from earthly mould;
    And hell itself will pass away,
And leave her dolorous mansions to the peering day.

    Yea, truth and justice then
    Will down return to men,
Orbed in a rainbow; and, like glories wearing,
    Mercy will sit between,
    Throned in celestial sheen,
With radiant feet the tissued clouds down steering;
    And heaven, as at some festival,
Will open wide the gates of her high palace hall.

But wisest Fate says No,
  This must not yet be so;
The Babe yet lies in smiling infancy,
  That on the bitter cross
  Must redeem our loss;
So both Himself and us to glorify:
Yet first, to those enchained in sleep,
The wakeful trump of doom must thunder through the deep.

With such a horrid clang
  As on Mount Sinai rang
While the red fire and smouldering clouds outbrake:
  The aged earth, aghast
  With terror of that blast,
Shall from the surface to the centre shake;
When, at the world's last session,
The dreadful Judge in middle air shall spread His throne.

And then at last our bliss
  Full and perfect is,
But now begins; for, from this happy day,
  The old dragon under ground,
  In straiter limits bound.
Not half so far casts his usurped sway;
And, wrath to see his kingdom fail,
Swinges the scaly horror of his folded tail.

The oracles are dumb,
  No voice or hideous hum
Runs through the archèd roof in words deceiving.
  Apollo from his shrine
  Can no more divine,

With hollow shriek the steep of Delphos leaving.
No nightly trance, or breathèd spell,
Inspires the pale-eyed priest from the prophetic cell.

    The lonely mountains o'er,
    And the resounding shore,
A voice of weeping heard and loud lament;
    From haunted spring and dale,
    Edgèd with poplar pale,
The parting genius is with sighing sent;
With flower-inwoven tresses torn,
The nymphs in twilight shade of tangled thickets mourn.

    In consecrated earth,
    And on the holy hearth,
The Lars and Lemures moan with midnight plaint;
    In urns, and altars round,
    A drear and dying sound
Affrights the Flamens at their service quaint;
And the chill marble seems to sweat,
While each peculiar power forgoes his wonted seat.

    Peor and Baalim
    Forsake their temples dim,
With that twice-battered god of Palestine;
    And moonèd Ashtaroth,
    Heaven's queen and mother both,
Now sits not girt with tapers' holy shine;
The Libyc Hammon shrinks his horn,
In vain the Tyrian maids their wounded Thammuz mourn.

    And sullen Moloch, fled,
    Hath left in shadows dread

His burning idol all of blackest hue;
  In vain with cymbals' ring,
  They call the grisly king,
In dismal dance about the furnace blue;
  The brutish gods of Nile as fast,
Isis, and Orus, and the dog Anubis, haste.

  Nor is Osiris seen
  In Memphian grove, or green,
Trampling the unshowered grass with lowings loud:
  Nor can he be at rest
  Within his sacred chest;
Nought but profoundest hell can be his shroud;
  In vain, with timbrelled anthems dark,
The sable-stoled sorcerers bear his worshipped ark.

  He feels from Judah's land
  The dreaded Infant's hand,
The rays of Bethlehem blind his dusky eyn;
  Nor all the gods beside
  Longer dare abide,
Not Typhon huge ending in snaky twine;
  Our Babe, to show His Godhead true,
Can in His swaddling bands control the damnéd crew.

  So, when the Sun in bed,
  Curtained with cloudy red,
Pillows his chin upon an orient wave,
  The flocking shadows pale
  Troop to the infernal jail,
Each fettered ghost slips to his several grave,
  And the yellow-skirted fays
Fly after the night-steeds, leaving their moon-loved maze.

But see, the Virgin blest
Hath laid her Babe to rest;
Time is, our tedious song should here have ending:
Heaven's youngest-teemèd star
Hath fixed her polished car,
Her sleeping Lord, with handmaid lamp, attending:
And all about the courtly stable
Bright-harnessed angels sit in order serviceable.

A Christmas Carol.

(SAMUEL T. COLERIDGE.)

THE shepherds went their hasty way,
    And found the lowly stable shed
Where the virgin mother lay :
    And now they checked their eager tread,
For, to the Babe that at her bosom clung,
A mother's song the virgin mother sung.

They told her how a glorious light,
    Streaming from a heavenly throng,
Around them shone, suspending night !
    While, sweeter than a mother's song,
Blest angels heralded the Saviour's birth,
Glory to God on high ! and peace on earth.

She listened to the tale divine,
    And closer still the Babe she pressed :
And while she cried, The Babe is mine !
    The milk rushed faster to her breast :
Joy rose within her, like a summer's morn ;
Peace, peace on earth ! the Prince of Peace is born.

Thou mother of the Prince of Peace,
    Poor, simple, and of low estate,
That strife should vanish, battle cease,
    O why should this thy soul elate ?
Sweet music's loudest note, the poet's story, —
Didst thou ne'er love to hear of fame and glory ?

And is not war a youthful king,
    A stately hero clad in mail?
Beneath his footsteps laurels spring;
    Him earth's majestic monarchs hail
Their friend, their playmate! and his bold bright eye
Compels the maiden's love-confessing sigh.

" Tell this in some more courtly scene,
    To maids and youths in robes of state!
I am a woman poor and mean,
    And, therefore, is my soul elate.
War is a ruffian, all with guilt defiled,
That from the aged father tears his child!

" A murderous fiend, by fiends adored,
    He kills the sire and starves the son;
The husband kills, and from her board
    Steals all his widow's toil had won!
Plunders God's world of beauty; rends away
All safety from the night, all comfort from the day.

" Then wisely is my soul elate,
    That strife should vanish, battle cease.
I'm poor and of a low estate,
    The mother of the Prince of Peace.
Joy rises in me, like a summer's morn:
Peace, peace on earth, the Prince of Peace is born."

Christmas Day.

(GEORGE WITHER)

As on the night before this happy morn,
 A blessed angel unto shepherds told,
Where (in a stable) He was poorly born,
 Whom nor the earth, nor heaven of heavens can hold
  Through Bethlem rung
   This news at their return ;
  Yea, angels sung
   That God with us was born ;
And they made mirth because we should not mourn.

 Their angel-carol sing we, then,
  To God on high all glory be,
  For peace on earth bestoweth He,
 And showeth favour unto men.

This favour Christ vouchsafed for our sake ;
 To buy us thrones, He in a manger lay ;
Our weakness took, that we His strength might take :
 And was disrobed that He might us array ;
  Our flesh He wore,
   Our sin to wear away ;
  Our curse He bore,
   That we escape it may ;
And wept for us, that we might sing for aye.

CHRISTMAS EVE AND CHRISTMAS DAY

With angels, therefore, sing again,
    To God on high all glory be;
      For peace on earth bestoweth He,
And showeth favour unto men.

A Christmas Hymn.

(ALFRED DOMETT.)

It was the calm and silent night!
    Seven hundred years and fifty-three,
Had Rome been growing up to might,
    And now was queen of land and sea!
No sound was heard of clashing wars—
    Peace brooded o'er the hushed domain;
Apollo, Pallas, Jove, and Mars,
    Held undisturbed their ancient reign,
      In the solemn midnight,
        Centuries ago!

'Twas in the calm and silent night!
    The Senator of haughty Rome,
Impatient urged his chariot's flight,
    From lordly revel rolling home!
Triumphal arches, gleaming, swell
    His breast with thoughts of boundless sway;
What recked the Roman what befell
    A paltry province far away,
      In the solemn midnight,
        Centuries ago!

Within that province far away,
   Went plodding home a weary boor;
A streak of light before him lay,
   Fallen through a half-shut stable-door
Across his path. He paused, for naught
   Told what was going on within:
How keen the stars! his only thought;
   The air how calm, and cold, and thin,
     In the solemn midnight,
      Centuries ago!

Oh, strange indifference!—low and high
   Drowsed over common joys and cares;
The earth was still, but knew not why;
   The world was listening—unawares!
How calm a moment may precede
   One that shall thrill the world forever!
To that still moment none would heed;
   Man's doom was linked, no more to sever,
     In the solemn midnight,
      Centuries ago!

It is the calm and silent night!
   A thousand bells ring out, and throw
Their joyous peals abroad, and smite
   The darkness—charmed and holy now!
The night that erst no shame had worn,
   To it a happier name is given;
For in the stable lay, new-born,
   The peaceful Prince of earth and heaven,
     In the solemn midnight,
      Centuries ago!

The Nativity.

NIGHT is set in, the stars their lamps are raising;
  Each dewy flower hath closed its perfumed chalice;
O'er the blue hills the city lights are blazing,
  And the gay cressets gleam in cot and palace.
Down the green sheep-tracks rest the flocks enfolden,
  Round their still cotes the hinds their fires are waking,
While in the homes of Bethlehem lie holden
  Eyes all unconscious of the mystery breaking.

      Oh, wonder of all wonders,
        The hinds their watch are keeping,
      A babe is in the manger—
        Christ Jesus there is sleeping;
      The oxen round Him lowing,
      The ass his forehead bowing.
      The maiden mother kneeling,
      While night is o'er them stealing.

Soon shall a fire-flood kindle up the horizon,
  Paling the night stars in their fairy shining.
Paling the broad sun at his first uprising,
  Paling the bright moon at his red declining.
Hark, through the opened lattice of Heaven's portals
  Soundeth—"To God be glory in the highest,
Peace be on earth; Good-will to loving mortals."
  Peace to thee, Christian, while with joy thou criest.

      Oh, wonder of all wonders,
        The hinds their watch are keeping,
      A babe is in the manger—
        Christ Jesus there is sleeping.

Christmas Carol.

(FELICIA HEMANS.)

O LOVELY voices of the sky,
  That hymned the Saviour's birth!
Are ye not singing still on high,
  Ye that sang, "Peace on earth?"
To us yet speak the strains,
  Wherewith, in days gone by,
Ye blessèd Syrian swains,
  O voices of the sky!

O clear and shining light, whose beams
  That hour heaven's glory shed
Around the palms, and o'er the streams,
  And on the shepherd's head;
Be near through life and death,
  As in that holiest night
Of Hope, and Joy, and Faith,
  O clear and shining light!

O star which led to Him, whose love
  Brought down man's ransom free;
Where art thou?—'midst the hosts above,
  May we still gaze on thee?—
In heaven thou art not set;
  Thy rays earth might not dim;—
Send them to guide us yet!
  O star which led to Him!

Poems on Winter.

WHEN icicles hang by the wall,
    And Dick the shepherd blows his nail,
And Tom bears logs into the hall,
    And milk comes frozen home in pail:

When blood is nipped, and ways be foul,
Then nightly sings the staring owl,
        To-whoo;
Tu-whit, to-whoo, a merry note,
While greasy Joan doth keel* the pot.

When all aloud the wind doth blow,
    And coughing drowns the parson's saw,
And birds sit brooding in the snow,
    And Marian's nose looks red and raw:
When roasted crabs hiss in the bowl,
Then nightly sings the staring owl,
        To-whoo;
Tu-whit, to-whoo, a merry note,
While greasy Joan doth keel the pot.

                              SHAKESPEARE.
            * Cool

NEXT came the chill December:
  Yet he, through merry feasting which he made,
And great bonfires, did not the cold remember;
  His Saviour's birth his mind so much did glad:
  Upon a shaggy-bearded goat he rode,
The same wherewith Dan Jove in tender years,
  They say, was nourished by th' Idæan maid;
And in his hand a broad deep bowl he bears,
Of which he freely drinks an health to all his peers.

Lastly, came Winter, clothèd all in frieze,
  Chattering his teeth for cold that did him chill;
Whilst on his hoary beard his breath did freeze,
  And the dull drops, that from his purpled bill,
  As from a limbeck, did adown distil:
In his right hand a tippèd staff he held,
  With which his feeble steps he stayèd still;
For he was faint with cold, and weak with eld,
That scarce his loosèd limbs he able was to wield.
                                        EDMUND SPENSER.

––––––––––

FAR from the track, and blest abode of man;
While round him night resistless closes fast,
And every tempest, howling o'er his head,
Renders the savage wilderness more wild.
*   *   *   *   *   Down he sinks
Beneath the shelter of the shapeless drift,
Thinking o'er all the bitterness of death,
Mix'd with the tender anguish nature shoots
Through the wrung bosom of the dying man.
*   *   *   *   *   *   *   *

Nor wife, nor children, more shall he behold,
Nor friends, nor sacred home.   On every nerve
The deadly winter seizes; shuts up sense;
And, o'er his inmost vitals creeping cold,
Lays him along the snows a stiffened corse—
Stretched out, and bleaching in the northern blast.
    Ah! little think the gay licentious proud,
Whom pleasure, power, and affluence, surround;
They, who their thoughtless hours in giddy mirth,
And wanton, often cruel, riot waste;
Ah! little think they, while they dance along,
How many feel, this very moment, death.
And all the sad variety of pain.

THOMSON.

O WINTER, ruler of the inverted year,
Thy scattered hair with sleet like ashes filled,
Thy breath congealed upon thy lips, thy cheeks
Fringed with a beard made white with other snows
Than those of age, thy forehead wrapped in clouds,
A leafless branch thy sceptre, and thy throne
A sliding car, indebted to no wheels,
But urged by storms along its slippery way,
I love thee, all unlovely as thou seem'st,
And dreaded as thou art! Thou hold'st the sun
A prisoner in the yet undawning east,
Shortening his journey between morn and noon,
And hurrying him, impatient of his stay,
Down to the rosy west; but kindly still
Compensating his loss with added hours
Of social converse and instructive ease,
And gathering, at short notice, in one group,
The family dispersed, and fixing thought,
Not less dispersed by daylight and its cares.
I crown thee king of intimate delights,
Fireside enjoyments, homeborn happiness,
And all the comforts that the lowly roof
Of undisturbed retirement, and the hours
Of long uninterrupted evening know.

WILLIAM COWPER.

A WRINKLED, crabbed man they picture thee,
    Old Winter, with a rugged beard as gray
As the long moss upon the apple-tree;
Blue lipt, an ice-drop at thy sharp blue nose:
    Close muffled up, and on thy dreary way,

Plodding alone through sleet and drifting snows.
They should have drawn thee by the high-heapt hearth,
  Old Winter! seated in thy great arm-chair,
Watching the children at their Christmas mirth,
  Or circled by them, as thy lips declare
Some merry jest, or tale of murder dire,
  Or troubled spirit that disturbs the night,
Pausing at times to rouse the mouldering fire,
Or taste the old October brown and bright.

ROBERT SOUTHEY.

—   ·

The Christmas Tree.

A MERRY, merry Christmas!
  To crown the closing year;
Peace and good-will to mortals,
  And words of holy cheer!

What though the dreary landscape
  Be robed in drifting snow,
If on the social hearthstone
  The Christmas fire may glow?

What though the wind at evening
  Blow harsh o'er land and sea,
If eager hands and joyful
  Light up the Christmas Tree?

Soft falls its pleasing lustre
  Upon the group around,—

The Christmas Tree.

A Christmas Carol.

On merry laughing childhood,
　And age with glory crowned.

With eyes of rapture beaming,
　Each little guest receives
Affection's token gleaming
　From out the shining leaves.

The grand-dame greets her children,
　And smiles their joy to see,
On Christmas eves of olden
　So eager once was she.

With peace serene and beautiful
　Her waning life shall shine,
As Christmas crowns the twelvemonths
　With light and joy divine.

———

A Christmas Carol.

From the Noel Bourguignon de Gui Barôzai.

(H. W. LONGFELLOW.)

I HEAR along our street
Pass the minstrel throngs;
Hark! they play so sweet,
On their hautboys, Christmas songs!
　　Let us by the fire
　　Ever higher
Sing them till the night expire!

In December ring
Every day the chimes;
Loud the gleemen sing
In the streets their merry rhymes.
Let us by the fire, etc.

Shepherds at the grange,
Where the Babe was born,
Sang, with many a change,
Christmas carols until morn.
Let us by the fire, etc.

These good people sang
Songs devout and sweet;
While the rafters rang,
There they stood with freezing feet.
Let us by the fire, etc.

Nuns in frigid cells
At this holy tide,
For want of something else,
Christmas songs at times have tried.
Let us by the fire, etc.

Washer-women old
To the sound they beat,
Sing by rivers cold,
With uncovered heads and feet.
Let us by the fire, etc,

Who by the fireside stands
Stamps his feet and sings;

Church Bells.

But he who blows his hands
Not so gay a carol brings.
Let us by the fire, etc.

Church Bells.

(JOHN KEBLE.)

WAKE me to-night, my mother dear
That I may hear
The Christmas Bells, so soft and clear,
To high and low glad tidings tell,
How God the Father loved us well;
How God the Eternal Son
Came to undo what we had done;
How God the Paraclete,
Who in the chaste womb formed the Babe so sweet,
In power and glory came, the birth to aid and greet.

Wake me, that I the twelvemonth long
May bear the song
About with me in the world's throng;
That treasured joys of Christmas tide
May with mine hour of gloom abide;
The Christmas Carol ring
Deep in my heart, when I would sing;
Each of the twelve good days
Its earnest yield of duteous love and praise,
Ensuring happy months, and hallowing common ways.

Wake me again, my mother dear,
That I may hear
The peal of the departing year.
O well I love, the step of Time
Should move to that familiar chime:
Fair fall the tones that steep
The Old Year in the dews of sleep,
The New guide softly in
With hopes to sweet, and memories akin!
Long may that soothing cadence ear, heart, conscience win.

A Visit from St. Nicholas.

(CLEMENT C. MOORE.)

Twas the night before Christmas, when all through the house
Not a creature was stirring, not even a mouse;
The stockings were hung by the chimney with care,
In hopes that St. Nicholas soon would be there;
The children were nestled all snug in their beds,
While visions of sugar-plums danced in their heads;
And mamma in her kerchief, and I in my cap,
Had just settled our brains for a long winter's nap—
When out on the lawn there rose such a clatter,
I sprang from my bed to see what was the matter.
Away to the window I flew like a flash,
Tore open the shutters and threw up the sash.
The moon, on the breast of the new-fallen snow,
Gave a lustre of mid-day to objects below;
When, what to my wondering eyes should appear,
But a miniature sleigh, and eight tiny rein-deer,

With a little old driver, so lively and quick,
I knew in a moment it must be St. Nick.
More rapid than eagles his coursers they came,
And he whistled, and shouted, and called them by name;
"Now, Dasher! now, Dancer! now, Prancer and Vixen!
On! Comet, on! Cupid, on! Dunder and Blitzen—
To the top of the porch, to the top of the wall!
Now, dash away, dash away, dash away all!"

As dry leaves that before the wild hurricane fly,
When they meet with an obstacle, mount to the sky,
So, up to the house-top the coursers they flew,
With a sleigh full of toys—and St. Nicholas too.
And then in a twinkling I heard on the roof,
The prancing and pawing of each little hoof.
As I drew in my head, and was turning around,
Down the chimney St. Nicholas came with a bound.
He was dressed all in fur from his head to his foot,
And his clothes were all tarnished with ashes and soot;
A bundle of toys he had flung on his back,
And he looked like a peddler just opening his pack.
His eyes how they twinkled! his dimples how merry!
His cheeks were like roses, his nose like a cherry;
His droll little mouth was drawn up like a bow,
And the beard on his chin was as white as the snow;
The stump of a pipe he held tight in his teeth,
And the smoke, it encircled his head like a wreath.
He had a broad face, and a little round belly,
That shook when he laughed, like a bowl full of jelly.
He was chubby and plump—a right jolly old elf;
And I laughed when I saw him, in spite of myself.
A wink of his eye, and a twist of his head,
Soon gave me to know I had nothing to dread.
He spoke not a word, but went straight to his work,
And filled all the stockings; then turned with a jerk,
And laying his finger aside of his nose,
And giving a nod, up the chimney he rose.
He sprang to his sleigh, to his team gave a whistle,
And away they all flew like the down of a thistle;
But I heard him exclaim, ere he drove out of sight,
"MERRY CHRISTMAS TO ALL, AND TO ALL A GOOD-NIGHT!"

The Death of the Old Year.

ALFRED TENNYSON.)

FULL knee-deep lies the winter snow,
  And the winter winds are wearily sighing:
Toll ye the church-bell sad and slow,
And tread softly, and speak low,
  For the Old Year lies a-dying.
    Old Year, you must not die;
    You came to us so readily,
    You lived with us so steadily,
    Old Year, you shall not die.

He lieth still: he doth not move:
  He will not see the dawn of day.
He hath no other life above.
He gave me a friend, and a true, true love,
  And the New Year will take 'em away.
    Old Year, you must not go;
    So long as you have been with us,
    Such joy as you have seen with us,
    Old Year, you shall not go.

He frothed his bumpers to the brim;
  A jollier year we shall not see.
But though his eyes are waxing dim,
And though his foes speak ill of him,
  He was a friend to me.
    Old Year, you shall not die;
    We did so laugh and cry with you.
    I've half a mind to die with you,
    Old Year, if you must die.

He was full of joke and jest,
  But all his merry quips are o'er.
To see him die, across the waste
His son and heir doth ride post haste,
  But he'll be dead before.
      Every one for his own.
      The night is starry and cold, my friend,
      And the New Year blithe and bold, my friend,
      Comes up to take his own.

How hard he breathes! over the snow
  I heard just now the crowing cock.
The shadows flicker to and fro:
The cricket chirps: the light burns low:
  'Tis nearly twelve o'clock.
      Shake hands, before you die.
      Old Year, we'll dearly rue for you:
      What is it we can do for you?
      Speak out before you die.

His face is growing sharp and thin.
  Alack, our friend is gone!
Close up his eyes: tie up his chin:
Step from the corpse, and let him in
  That standeth there alone,
      And waiteth at the door.
      There's a new foot on the floor, my friend,
      And a new face at the door, my friend,
      A new face at the door.

www.ingramcontent.com/pod-product-compliance
Lightning Source LLC
Chambersburg PA
CBHW020802020726
47495CB00008B/2547